D0624129

This book belongs to:

_____

To Kate and Patrick for trusting me . . .
and Mark for understanding my passion
—Mandy Sutcliffe

Text copyright © 2016 by Mark Sperring
Jacket art and interior illustrations copyright © 2016 by Mandy Sutcliffe

All rights reserved. Published in the United States by Random House Children's Books,
a division of Penguin Random House LLC, New York.
Originally published in Great Britain by Orchard Books, London, in 2015.

Random House and the colophon are registered trademarks of Penguin Random House LLC.

Visit us on the Web! randomhousekids.com

Educators and librarians, for a variety of teaching tools, visit us at RHTeachersLibrarians.com

Library of Congress Cataloging-in-Publication Data is available upon request.

ISBN 978-0-399-54947-2 (trade) —ISBN 978-0-399-54949-6 (ebook)

MANUFACTURED IN CHINA
10 9 8 7 6 5 4 3 2 1
First Edition

Random House Children's Books supports the First Amendment
and celebrates the right to read.

Hop Along Boo

Time For Bed

Mandy Sutcliffe

With words by Mark Sperring

RANDOM HOUSE 🏠 NEW YORK

THE MOON PEEPS bright through the window.

The stars razzle-dazzle on high.

Boo, can you hear someone singing?

Belle's singing a lullaby!

She's strumming a sleepy old song now,
Singing, "Boo, it's time for your bed!"
So, Boo, don't you bunny around now.
The pillow's awaiting your head!

The whole world is snug in their jammies.
They've all brushed their teeth till they gleam.
They're all skipping out of the bathroom,
And heading off into a dream.

The cowboys way out on the prairie

Have wished all their horses good night.

They're climbing the stairs up to bed now,
While holding their teddy bears tight!

The dancers have hung up their shoes now.
Their pliés have all had to stop.

So, Boo, point your toes toward bed now,
And spring up those stairs with a hop!

The fairies all flew up so lightly,
Wings glittering in the moon's soft glow · · ·

. . . But the elephants' feet thumped like thunder.

I don't think they wanted to go!

All the babies are snug in their cribs now,
As comfy as babies can be.
The toddlers have all toddled off now—
Just in time for a story . . . or three!

All the big ships have dropped anchor—sploosh!

Little sailors are resting their heads.

Pirates are snoozing in hammocks.

Captain Boo, now it's time for bed!

So, Boo, there's no time for games now,
For most of the world's fast asleep.
And Belle's little song has turned into a . . .

. . . YAAAAAAAAAAAWN!

So hop to it, Boo.

Move those feet!

Bedtime and blankets are waiting.

Cuddles and snuggles are too.

On a pillow as soft as a feather,

Let's whisper . . .

. . . "Good night. I love you."